This book belongs to

Sandy Creek
122 Fifth Avenue
New York, NY 10011

ISBN 978-1-4351-1922-2

10 9 8 7 6 5 4 3 2 Lot
Manufactured 8/18/2010
Manufactured in China

The Secret Garden

Written by Frances Hodgson Burnett
Retold by Gaby Goldsack
Illustrated by Simon Anderson

Sandy Creek

When Mary Lennox first arrived at Misselthwaite Manor, she was sickly-looking and bad-tempered. She had been born in India, where she had often been ill and always been ignored by her parents. Then her parents had died of a terrible illness and Mary had been whisked away to live with her uncle in the north of England.

Uncle Archibald Craven had a crooked back and was very grumpy. He'd never been the same since his wife had died many years ago. He wasn't at all interested in Mary and spent most of his time abroad.

On her first day at Misselthwaite Manor, Mary was shown to her room and told to mind her own business and not poke around.

The next morning, Mary was awoken by Martha, the maid. Martha was cheerful and very talkative.

Suddenly, Mary felt very lonely and burst into tears.

"You mustn't cry like that," begged Martha. She sounded so kind, that Mary stopped crying and began to listen to her cheerful chatter. Martha told Mary all about the moors, the garden and her brother Dickon.

"Dickon plays on the moors for hours. He makes friends with the animals," said Martha. "Now why don't you go into the garden, and play?"

At first Mary wasn't interested in going out to play. But when she heard more about Dickon and his animal friends, she decided to go out. As she wrapped up warm, Martha told her about a garden that had been locked up since Mr. Craven's wife had died. It had been Mrs. Craven's special garden. After she had died, Mr. Craven had buried the key and no one had been there since.

When she was outside, Mary couldn't help thinking about the locked garden. She wondered where it was. As she looked around, she met a gardener called Ben. At first, Ben was very grumpy but when he saw how lonely Mary was he became friendly. He even introduced Mary to his tame robin.

"He lives in the locked garden," Ben explained. But when Mary asked more about the garden, he marched off.

After that first day, Mary went out into the garden each day. It was winter, so she ran around to keep warm. Slowly, she grew stronger and became less bad tempered.

One day, Mary was watching the robin in the garden when she saw him hopping around something.

It was a rusty old key.
Mary picked it up.
"Perhaps it's the key to
the locked garden,"
she whispered.

"Now I just need to find the door it unlocks."
The next day, Mary was talking to her friend
the robin, when a gust of wind blew some
ivy from a wall and a door was revealed.
She tried the key in the lock and the door
swung open. Mary slipped through the door.
She was standing inside the secret garden. It
was overgrown and tangled but very beautiful.

Mary walked around and saw that tiny flowers were trying to poke through the weeds. She set to work at once. She dug and weeded with a stick. After that, Mary went to work in the secret garden every day.

One day, Mary asked Martha where she could get some seeds and tools. She didn't tell her about the secret garden. She just said that she wanted a patch of garden for herself. Martha said that Dickon could get her what she wanted, so Mary sat down and wrote him a note.

A few days later, Mary was playing in the big garden when she met a boy surrounded by wild animals. It was Dickon. He'd brought her the things she'd asked for.

Dickon was so friendly that Mary quickly found herself showing him the secret garden. Like Mary, he soon fell in love with it. And from that day on, they both worked really hard to restore the garden.

Whilst Mary enjoyed the garden, much of the house remained a mystery to her. At night, she often thought she heard somebody crying. One night, she decided to get up and find out where the sound was coming from. She wandered along unfamiliar corridors, until she saw a light coming from beneath a door.

She pushed the door open and discovered a boy inside.

"Who are you?" demanded the boy.

"I'm Mary," she replied. "Who are you?"

"I'm Colin Craven. Mr. Craven's son," said the boy.

Colin explained that he was ill and didn't like being seen. He told Mary that when he grew up he was going to have a crooked back just like his father and that he couldn't walk and was going to die. His father didn't visit him very often because Colin reminded him of his dead wife.

Mary and Colin talked and talked. He listened eagerly as she told him all about Dickon and the garden. Before long, they had become great friends.

Martha and the other servants were quite angry when they discovered that Mary had found out about Colin. But when they saw how happy Colin was, they forgave her.

Mary visited Colin every day. Colin refused to go outside because he felt so sorry for himself. Sometimes he even flew into furious rages.

One day, Colin and Mary had a fight because she was spending so much time with Dickon who he hadn't met. Colin threw a pillow at Mary and told her to leave his room.

Later Colin threw a tantrum. He screamed and screamed. Nobody knew what to do. Eventually, Mary rushed into his room. She stamped her foot and told him to stop.

"I felt a lump on my back. I'm going to die," sobbed Colin.

"No you're not," said Mary. And she found a mirror to show him that his back was fine.

When Colin had calmed down, he told Mary that he wanted to meet Dickon and visit the secret garden.

Dickon was brought around to meet Colin. He carried a newborn lamb in his arms. Colin stared at him in delight. Then, they started to talk. Soon they were planning how Colin could visit the secret garden without anyone knowing.

A few days later, Colin was carried downstairs and put in a wheelchair. Dickon pushed the wheelchair while Mary walked at their side. They walked through the big garden and then, when no one was looking, slipped into the secret garden. Colin looked around and gasped with delight. Sun fell on his face and color flowed into his pale cheeks.

"I shall get well! I shall get well!" he cried. "Mary! Dickon! I shall get well! And I shall live for ever and ever and ever!"

Colin watched as Mary and Dickon dug and weeded.

"I don't want this afternoon to end," said Colin. "But I shall come back tomorrow and the day after, and the day after."

"We'll have you walking around and digging before long," said Dickon.

"There's nothing wrong with my legs," said Colin. "But they are so thin and weak I'm afraid to stand on them."

"When you stop being afraid, you'll stand on them," smiled Dickon.

They all sat in the sun, until Colin suddenly shouted out, "Who is that man peering over the wall?" Mary and Dickon looked around to see Ben glaring at them from the top of the ladder. He shook an angry fist at Mary.

"How dare you..." he began, before spotting Colin. "Hey, you're the poor crippled boy," he said.

"I'm not crippled!" cried Colin. He was so angry that, using all his strength, he caught hold of Dickon's arm and pulled himself to his feet.

"You can walk!" exclaimed Ben. "You're not going to die."

Colin stood straighter and straighter. "I'm your master when my father's away," he said. "Don't tell anyone about seeing us here."

Ben disappeared behind the wall.

Colin remained standing. Then, holding on to Dickon's arm, he walked a few steps. He was still standing when Ben walked through the door.

"This was my mother's garden, wasn't it?" Colin asked him.

"Yes," said Ben. "I climb over the wall from time to time to look after it. I don't get in as often as I'd like because it's hard to climb over the wall."

Colin sat down and picked up a spade. He began to dig, then turned around to Dickon.

"You said I would walk and dig," he smiled. "And look, I'm doing both."

After that, Colin and Mary returned to the garden each day. And as the secret garden bloomed, so did Colin.

Every day, Colin practiced walking. Slowly he grew stronger. But he didn't want everyone to know and made Mary, Dickon, and Ben promise to keep it a secret.

"One day I will walk into Father's study and surprise him," he told them.

Meanwhile, Mr. Craven, Colin's father, was traveling abroad when he had a dream. In the dream he saw the ghost of his wife in her beloved garden. When he awoke, he knew that he must return to Misselthwaite Manor and open up the locked garden.

A few days later, Mr. Craven was at Misselthwaite once more. He walked through the grounds. As he approached his wife's hidden garden, he heard the sound of running feet and childish laughter. Suddenly, the ivy-covered door swung open and out burst a young boy. He was tall and handsome. It was Colin. Colin was very surprised to see his father.

"Father," he said. "I'm Colin. You can't believe it. I scarcely can myself. It was the garden that did it—and Mary and Dickon."

Mr. Craven's heart sang with joy. His son was a healthy young boy. He hugged Colin and then followed him through the door. And there, Colin, Mary, and Dickon showed him the magic of the secret garden.